U0007725

我對牠比對其他爬蟲動物更感到好奇。
牠有著凌亂的頭髮和藍色的眼睛，沒有屁股，
身材逐漸變細、像根蘿蔔，當牠站起身、伸展四肢時，就像一輛起重機！

星期六

SATURDAY

我來到這兒差不多有一天了，我昨天到達的，似乎是這樣吧！
因為如果有前天，那麼當它發生時，我還不在，否則我應該記得。
當然，也有可能真有那一天，但我沒注意到！

沒關係，從現在開始，我會非常的留心一切事物，
假如還有任何「前天」發生，我一定會把它們記錄下來。
而且最好一開始就做對，不要把那些紀錄弄亂了。
我有種預感，這些細節
有一天會成為歷史學家非常重要的資料。

I am almost a whole day old, now. I arrived yesterday.
That is as it seems to me. And it must be so, for if there was a
day-before-yesterday I was not there when it happened, or I
should remember it. It could be, of course, that it did happen,
and that I was not noticing.

Very well; I will be very watchful now, and if any day-before-
yesterdays happen I will make a note of it. It will be best to start
right and not let the record get confused, for some instinct tells
me that these details are going to be important to the historian
some day.

我覺得像是一種實驗，
我真的覺得自己就像是一個實驗品，
沒有別人比我更像實驗品了，
因此我很努力地說服自己就是一個實驗品，
除此之外，什麼都不是。

For I feel like an experiment,
I feel exactly like an experiment; it would be impossible for a
person to feel more like an experiment than I do,
and so I am coming to feel convinced that that is what I AM——
an experiment; just an experiment, and nothing more.

—

不過如果我是一項實驗，那這項實驗只有我嗎？

不，我並不這樣覺得，我認為其餘的也是實驗的部份。

或許我是這實驗最主要的部份，

但我想其他的部份應該也參與其中。

我的身份是確認無虞的嗎？

還是必須要小心翼翼的注意呢？

我想答案可能是後者。

有些直覺告訴我，永遠的保有警惕之心將是保有主權的代價。

（我覺得這真是一句很棒的諺語，至少對我這樣年輕的人而言）。

每件事情看起來都比昨天好。

—

Then if I am an experiment, am I the whole of it? No, I think
not; I think the rest of it is part of it.
I am the main part of it, but I think the rest of it has its share in
the matter.
Is my position assured, or do I have to watch it and take care of
it? The latter, perhaps.
Some instinct tells me that eternal vigilance is the price of
supremacy.
[That is a good phrase, I think, for one so young.]
Everything looks better today than it did yesterday.

因為趕著完成「昨天」，
山巒看起來凌亂又不協調，
平原則滿是垃拾和不要的東西，
這樣的景況讓人覺得哀傷。

高貴美麗的藝術品不應該被粗製濫造，
而這個宏偉的新世界
的確是一件高貴又美麗的藝術創作並且近乎完美，
雖然時間這麼短促。

In the rush of finishing up yesterday,
the mountains were left in a ragged condition,
and some of the plains were so cluttered with rubbish
and remnants that the aspects were quite distressing.

Noble and beautiful works of art should not be subjected to
haste; and this majestic new world is indeed a most noble
and beautiful work. And certainly marvelously near to being
perfect, notwithstanding the shortness of the time.

—

有些地方的星星太多，有些地方的星星卻不夠，
但毫無疑問的，這些問題很快就可被改善。
昨天晚上月亮鬆脫了，
它滑下並脫落到框架外 —— 一個非常嚴重的損失，
這讓我覺得好心痛。
在所有的裝飾品裡，
沒有任何東西比得上月亮的完美和美麗。
應該把它綁得更好些，
如果我們可以把它找回來。

—

There are too many stars in some places and not enough in others,
but that can be remedied presently, no doubt.
The moon got loose last night,
and slid down and fell out of the scheme —— a very great loss;
it breaks my heart to think of it.
There isn't another thing among the ornaments and decorations
that is comparable to it for beauty and finish.
It should have been fastened better.
If we can only get it back again.

但是沒有人知道月亮到哪裡去了，
而且不論是誰撿到它，就會把它藏起來，
我知道，是因為我就會這樣做。

我相信在其他事情上，我可以非常誠實。
但我已經開始體認到自己的天性是愛好美麗的，
對美麗的事物有極大的熱情。
所以最好別讓我保管月亮，那是不安全的。

But of course there is no telling where it went to.
And besides, whoever gets it will hide it;
I know it because I would do it myself.

I believe I can be honest in all other matters,
but I already begin to realize that the core and
center of my nature is love of the beautiful,
a passion for the beautiful, and that it would not
be safe to trust me with a moon that belonged to
another person and that person didn't know I had
it.

假如是在白天找到月亮，我會把它交出來，
因為我擔心會被發現，但若是在晚上找到它，
我一定會找些藉口不把它交出來。
因為我實在太喜歡月亮了，它們這麼漂亮又浪漫，
我希望我們可以有五個或者六個月亮，
那我就不用上床睡覺，
可以永遠不覺得疲倦、躺在鋪滿苔蘚的岸邊看著它們。

I could give up a moon that I found in the daytime, because I
should be afraid some one was looking; but if I found it in the
dark, I am sure I should find some kind of an excuse for not
saying anything about it.
For I do love moons, they are so pretty and so romantic.
I wish we had five or six; I would never go to bed; I should never
get tired lying on the moss-bank and looking up at them.

星星也很棒！
我希望能拿些星星放在我的頭髮上，
但我猜想永遠沒辦法這麼做。
如果你知道那些星星離我們有多遠，
一定會覺得很驚訝。
因為它們看起來並沒有那麼遙遠。

當它們昨晚第一次出現時，
我試著用一根竿子想將它們打落一些，
但卻搆不著它們，這讓我很吃驚。
然後我丟石塊把它們打下來，
丟到我覺得累了，
仍然一個也打不到。

或許因為我是左撇子，所以總是丟不好，
即便我瞄準那個不想要的目標，看會不會誤打誤中，
還是丟不到，即便已經快要打到了。
我看到那些黑壓壓的石塊
滑入那群金光閃閃的星星當中四十或五十次，
雖然有些看來快要接近了，最後仍是一無所獲。
或許如果再堅持一下，我就可以有一顆星星了。

Stars are good, too. I wish I could get some to put in my hair. But I suppose I never can. You would be surprised to find how far off they are, for they do not look it.

When they first showed, last night, I tried to knock some down with a pole, but it didn't reach, which astonished me; then I tried clods till I was all tired out, but I never got one.

It was because I am left-handed and cannot throw good. Even when I aimed at the one I wasn't after I couldn't hit the other one, though I did make some close shots, for I saw the black blot of the clod sail right into the midst of the golden clusters forty or fifty times, just barely missing them, and if I could have held out a little longer maybe I could have got one.

我哭了一會兒，
我想，以我的年齡來看，
這樣的行徑很合理。
稍微休息一下後，我拿了一個籃子，
開始前往這個圈子的最邊緣，
在那裡，星星更靠近地面，
我用雙手就可以拿到它們，
總之，這樣的方法會更好，
因為我可以輕易地就收集到那些星星，
而不會把它們弄破。

不過那裡比我所想像的還遙遠很多，
最後我還是放棄了，
我實在累到連一步也邁不出去，
而且雙腳又痛又受傷了。

So I cried a little, which was natural, I suppose, for one of my age, and after I was rested I got a basket and started for a place on the extreme rim of the circle, where the stars were close to the ground and I could get them with my hands, which would be better, anyway, because I could gather them tenderly then, and not break them.

But it was farther than I thought, and at last I had go give it up; I was so tired I couldn't drag my feet another step; and besides, they were sore and hurt me very much.

我沒辦法回家，
因為回家的路太遠，天氣也變冷了。
不過我發現了幾隻老虎，便睡在牠們之間，
那真是非常的舒服，
牠們的氣息也讓人感覺非常愉悅並甜美，
因為牠們是以草莓為生。
我以前從來沒有看過老虎，
但是一看見牠們身上的條紋，我就認出了牠們。
如果我也有像牠們一樣的皮毛，
就可以做一件很漂亮的大衣。

I couldn't get back home; it was too far, and turning cold; but
I found some tigers, and nestled in among them and was most
adorably comfortable, and their breath was sweet and pleasant,
because they live on strawberries.
I had never seen a tiger before, but I knew them in a minute by the
stripes.
If I could have one of those skins, it would make a lovely gown.

今天我對距離更有概念了。

每一個漂亮的東西，我都很希望能擁有，

便會很急切地想要伸手去抓取，有時候它們實在太遠了；

有時它們看來似乎離我一呎遠，

事實上卻只離我六吋的距離──

唉，中間還滿是荊棘。

從這些經驗和教訓中，我上了一堂課並領悟出一個道理，

「被刮傷的實驗品，要避開荊棘」，

我想對於像我這樣年紀輕的人而言，這是一句非常好的格言。

Today I am getting better ideas about distances.
I was so eager to get hold of every pretty thing that I
giddily grabbed for it, sometimes when it was too far
off, and sometimes when it was but six inches away but
seemed a foot——alas, with thorns between!
I learned a lesson; also I made an axiom, all out of my
own head——my very first one; THE SCRATCHED
EXPERIMENT SHUNS THE THORN.
I think it is a very good one for one so young.

昨天下午我跟著另一個實驗品，
保持著一個距離，想弄清楚牠到底是什麼用途，
但我沒辦法確認，
我想那是一個男人，
我從來沒看過男人，
但牠看起來像是一個男人，我想牠是，
我覺得那就像一個男人。

我發覺自己對牠，
比對其他的爬蟲動物更感到好奇。
如果牠是一種爬蟲類，我猜想牠是；
因為牠有著凌亂的頭髮和藍色的眼睛，
看起來就像一種爬蟲類動物。
牠沒有屁股，
身材逐漸變細、像根蘿蔔，
當牠站起身、伸展四肢時，
就像一輛起重機。
所以我認為牠是一種爬蟲類，
雖然牠也可能是一棟建築物。

I followed the other Experiment around, yesterday afternoon,
at a distance, to see what it might be for, if I could.
But I was not able to make out. I think it is a man.
I had never seen a man, but it looked like one,
and I feel sure that that is what it is.

I realize that I feel more curiosity about it than about any of
the other reptiles.
If it is a reptile, and I suppose it is;
for it has frowzy hair and blue eyes, and looks like a reptile.
It has no hips; it tapers like a carrot; when it stands,
it spreads itself apart like a derrick; so I think it is a reptile,
though it may be architecture.

剛開始我很怕牠，
每次當牠一轉身，我就逃跑，
因為我覺得牠要追我。
但是很快的，我發現牠只是試著想要離開，
後來我便不再膽怯，
而且在離牠二十碼左右的距離跟著牠好幾個小時，
我的行為讓牠覺得很緊張且不開心，
最後牠非常擔心並爬上一棵樹。
我在樹下等了一會兒後，
就放棄回家了。
今天又發生同樣的狀況，
我又把牠趕到樹上了。

———

I was afraid of it at first, and started to run every time it turned around, for I thought it was going to chase me; but by and by I found it was only trying to get away, so after that I was not timid any more, but tracked it along, several hours, about twenty yards behind, which made it nervous and unhappy.
At last it was a good deal worried, and climbed a tree.
I waited a good while, then gave it up and went home.
Today the same thing over. I've got it up the tree again.

星期天

—

SUNDAY

—

牠還是待在樹上，顯然牠是在休息。
不過那是一個藉口，
星期天並不是休息的日子，星期六才是。
看起來跟我相像的這個生物，對於休息的興趣遠大於其他的事情，
但如果要我這麼長時間都在休息，我一定會覺得很累；
光是要我坐著、看看樹，我就覺得很累。
我真想知道牠到底有什麼用途，我從沒看到牠做任何事。

It is up there yet. Resting, apparently. But that is a
subterfuge: Sunday isn't the day of rest; Saturday is
appointed for that.
It looks to me like a creature that is more interested in
resting than it anything else. It would tire me to rest so
much.
It tires me just to sit around and watch the tree. I do
wonder what it is for; I never see it do anything.

——

昨天晚上月亮被歸還了，我真的「太」高興了！
我想那些人還真誠實。
不過月亮又再度從天空滑落了，但我不覺得難過了。
當我有這種誠實的鄰居，根本不需要擔心，
牠們會把月亮歸還的；
我希望自己能做些什麼表示我的感激。
我想送一些星星給牠們，
因為我們不需要有這麼多。
我是指我，而不是我們，
我想那個爬行類動物根本不會在意這些事情。

——

They returned the moon last night, and I was SO happy!
I think it is very honest of them. It slid down and fell off again, but
I was not distressed; there is no need to worry when one has that
kind of neighbors; they will fetch it back.
I wish I could do something to show my appreciation. I would like
to send them some stars, for we have more than we can use.
I mean I, not we, for I can see that the reptile cares nothing for
such things.

——

牠沒什麼品味，又不怎麼仁慈。
昨天傍晚當我到那裡，牠趁著暮色躡手躡腳地爬下樹，
想要抓池塘中游來游去的斑紋魚，
我只好拿石塊丟牠，再把牠趕回樹上，
才能讓那些魚兒不被打擾。
我在想，「那」就是牠的用途嗎？牠沒有良心嗎？
牠對那些小生物都沒有一點憐憫之心嗎？
牠被設計並製造出來，就是為了做這樣粗魯的事情嗎？
牠看起來就是那樣的生物。

——

It has low tastes, and is not kind. When I went there yesterday
evening in the gloaming it had crept down and was trying to catch
the little speckled fishes that play in the pool, and I had to clod it
to make it go up the tree again and let them alone.
I wonder if THAT is what it is for? Hasn't it any heart? Hasn't it
any compassion for those little creatures? Can it be that it was
designed and manufactured for such ungentle work? It has the
look of it.

有一個石塊丟到了牠的耳後，
牠說了些話，這讓我很激動。
這是除了我自己外，第一次聽到語言。
我沒聽懂牠說的話，但牠似乎要表達什麼。
當我發現牠會說話，我對牠又重燃興趣了，
我非常喜歡說話，整天都在說話，
連睡夢中也可以。
我的話非常有趣，
如果有另一個人可以跟我說話，
那會更有趣，
如果想要，我可以一直不停地說下去。

One of the clods took it back of the ear, and it used language.
It gave me a thrill, for it was the first time I had ever heard speech, except my own.
I did not understand the words, but they seemed expressive.
When I found it could talk I felt a new interest in it, for I love to talk; I talk, all day, and in my sleep, too, and I am very interesting, but if I had another to talk to I could be twice as interesting, and would never stop, if desired.

如果這個爬行類動物是一個人，
那牠就不是「牠」，
那是不合乎文法的，不是嗎？
我想應該稱呼「他」，我這樣覺得。
我們可以這樣解析：主格是「他」；與格是「他」；
所有格是「他的」。
總之，在還沒證明牠是其他生物前，
就當牠是人，以「他」來稱呼吧。
這會比有那麼多的不確定性簡單多了！

If this reptile is a man, it isn't an IT, is it? That wouldn't be grammatical, would it? I think it would be HE.

I think so. In that case one would parse it thus: nominative, HE; dative, HIM; possessive, HIS'N.

Well, I will consider it a man and call it he until it turns out to be something else.

This will be handier than having so many uncertainties.

下周日

NEXT WEEK SUNDAY

一整個星期我都跟在他身後，
並試著更了解他。
他很害羞，所以我必須主動跟他說話，
但我並不在意這樣做。
他似乎對於我在他身旁覺得開心，
而我也使用「我們」這個友善的字眼，
因為這似乎可以讓他覺得有被認同的喜悅。

All the week I tagged around after him
and tried to get acquainted.
I had to do the talking, because he was shy,
but I didn't mind it.
He seemed pleased to have me around,
and I used the sociable "we" a good deal,
because it seemed to flatter him to be included.

星期三

WEDNESDAY

現在我們的確相處得很好，
而且也越來越熟悉彼此。
他不再試著避開我，這是一個好現象，
並顯示他喜歡我跟他在一起。
這讓我很高興，而我也研究如何在能力範圍內，
在每一個地方對他都能有所幫助，
以增加他對我的重視。
最近這陣子，
我替他把所有命名的工作都完成了，
讓他減輕了很大的負擔。
他對命名這檔事完全沒有天分，
顯而易見的，他非常感激我的所做所為。
但我並沒有讓他看出我知道他有這方面的弱點。
每當遇到一個新的生物，
我會搶在他陷入尷尬的靜默前想出名字，
以這種方式免去他不少尷尬的時刻。

We are getting along very well indeed, now,
and getting better and better acquainted.
He does not try to avoid me any more, which is a good sign,
and shows that he likes to have me with him.
That pleases me, and I study to be useful to him in every way
I can, so as to increase his regard.
During the last day or two I have taken all the work of
naming things off his hands, and this has been a great relief
to him, for he has no gift in that line, and is evidently very
grateful.
He can't think of a rational name to save him, but I do not let
him see that I am aware of his defect.
Whenever a new creature comes along I name it before he has
time to expose himself by an awkward silence.
In this way I have saved him many embarrassments.

—

我並沒有像他這樣的弱點。
只要一看到一隻動物，我就可以知道牠是什麼。
我並不需要想一下，那個動物的名字就會立刻出現在我的腦海中。
那就像是一種靈感，毫無疑問的，它就是一種靈感。
我很確定在半分鐘以前，我的腦海中完全沒有這些名字，
似乎光從那些生物的形態和行動的樣子，
我就能知道那些生物是什麼！

—

I have no defect like his. The minute I set eyes on an
animal I know what it is.
I don't have to reflect a moment; the right name
comes out instantly, just as if it were an inspiration,
as no doubt it is, for I am sure it wasn't in me half a
minute before.
I seem to know just by the shape of the creature
and the way it acts what animal it is.

當多多鳥出現時，

他認為牠是一隻野貓——我從他的雙眼中看出他是這麼想的！

但是我解救了他，我非常小心的不要傷到他的自尊。我只是開心的以一種平靜自然的語氣說道，「嗯，這不是多多鳥嗎？」

我解釋——但不顯露出解釋的語氣——我是如何知道多多鳥，雖然我想他可能因為我知道這個生物，而他不知道，會有一點不高興，不過很顯然他很羨慕我，那讓我很開心。每次在睡前只要一想到這件事，就讓我覺得很高興。即便是很小的事情，當我們覺得這是自己努力達成的成果，也會覺得非常的開心！

When the dodo came along he thought it was a wildcat —— I saw it in his eye. But I saved him. And I was careful not to do it in a way that could hurt his pride. I just spoke up in a quite natural way of pleased surprise, and not as if I was dreaming of conveying information, and said, "Well, I do declare, if there isn't the dodo!"

I explained —— without seeming to be explaining —— how I knew it for a dodo, and although I thought maybe he was a little piqued that I knew the creature when he didn't, it was quite evident that he admired me. That was very agreeable, and I thought of it more than once with gratification before I slept. How little a thing can make us happy when we feel that we have earned it!

星期四

THURSDAY

我第一次感到難過。
昨天他避開我，而且似乎希望我能夠不要跟他說話。
我真是難以相信，覺得一定是哪裡有問題。
我這麼喜歡跟他在一起，這麼喜歡跟他交談，
到底是怎麼回事？
我什麼也沒有做，他怎麼能這麼殘忍的對待我？

My first sorrow. Yesterday he avoided me and seemed to wish I would not talk to him.
I could not believe it, and thought there was some mistake,
for I loved to be with him, and loved to hear him talk,
and so how could it be that he could feel unkind toward me when I had not done anything?

41

——

不過最終這似乎是真的，
所以我離開並一個人孤單的坐在
我們被創造的那個早上，我第一次看到他的地方。
那時我不知道他是什麼，對他也很冷漠，
但現在這卻成了一個傷心地，每樣東西都讓我想起他。
我的心很痛。
我不是很清楚為什麼會這樣，
這是一種新的感覺，我以前從來沒有這種經驗，
那是一種神祕卻難以理解的感覺。

——

But at last it seemed true, so I went away and sat lonely in the
place where I first saw him the morning that we were made and
I did not know what he was and was indifferent about him; but
now it was a mournful place, and every little think spoke of him,
and my heart was very sore.
I did not know why very clearly, for it was a new feeling; I had
not experienced it before, and it was all a mystery, and I could not
make it out.

但是當夜晚來臨，
我難以忍受這種寂寞，
便跑到他新搭建的休息處去問他，
我做錯了什麼，
要怎麼樣補救，才可再度得到他親切的對待，
可是他卻把我趕到雨中，
這是我第一次覺得哀傷。

But when night came I could not bear the lonesomeness,
and went to the new shelter which he has built,
to ask him what I had done that was wrong and how I could
mend it and get back his kindness again;
but he put me out in the rain, and it was my first sorrow.

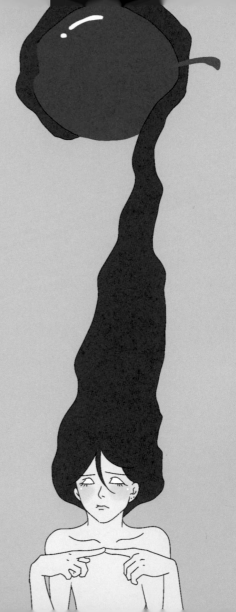

星期日
——

SUNDAY
——

現在又再度放晴了，我很開心！
而過去那些不開心的事情，我就盡量避免想它！
我想要摘一些蘋果給他，但一直丟不準，
不過我想我的好意會讓他覺得開心！
那些蘋果是被禁止摘取的，
他跟我說過，如果去摘那些蘋果，我就會面臨危險，
但是如果因為能讓他開心而遇到危險，
危險又算什麼呢？

It is pleasant again, now, and I am happy; but those were heavy days; I do not think of them when I can help it.
I tried to get him some of those apples, but I cannot learn to throw straight. I failed, but I think the good intention pleased him.
They are forbidden, and he says I shall come to harm; but so I come to harm through pleasing him, why shall I care for that harm?

星期一

MONDAY

今天早上我告訴他我的名字，
希望他會有興趣，但他一點也不關心。
這真是奇怪，
如果是他告訴我他的名字，我會很關心，
我想這會比任何其他的聲音都讓我開心。

This morning I told him my name, hoping it would
interest him. But he did not care for it. It is strange.
If he should tell me his name, I would care.
I think it would be pleasanter in my ears than any
other sound.

他不常說話，
或許是因為他並不聰明，所以想隱藏自己。
他會這樣想實在太可憐了，聰不聰明並不代表什麼，
人的價值之所在，是在於每個人的內心。
我希望能讓他了解，
唯有充滿善心和愛的心靈才是富足的，並且就足夠了，
缺少愛和善心，即便聰明，卻是貧困的！

He talks very little.
Perhaps it is because he is not bright, and is sensitive about it and
wishes to conceal it. It is such a pity that he should feel so, for
brightness is nothing; it is in the heart that the values lie.
I wish I could make him understand that a loving good heart is
riches, and riches enough, and that without it intellect is poverty.

雖然他很少說話，卻知道相當多的詞彙。
今天早上他就用了一個令人非常吃驚的好字眼。
很明顯的，他也發現到自己用了一個好字眼，
所以後來又用了那個字眼兩次。
他表現得不是很有技巧，
卻顯示出他擁有一定程度上的認知。
毫無疑問的，假如種子有被灌溉，便可以繼續成長。
他是從哪裡知道那些字？我不認為我使用過它。

Although he talks so little, he has quite a considerable vocabulary.
This morning he used a surprisingly good word.
He evidently recognized, himself, that it was a good one, for he
worked in in twice afterwards, casually.
It was not good casual art, still it showed that he possesses a
certain quality of perception.
Without a doubt that seed can be made to grow, if cultivated.
Where did he get that word? I do not think I have ever used it.

他對我的名字一點也不感興趣，
我試著掩飾失望，但失敗了。
於是我走開並坐在鋪滿苔癬的水邊，
把雙腳放進水中。
當我渴望有人可以看我、
有人可以說話時，
我就會來到這裡。
雖然池子裡那雪白、可愛的身體
並不足以安慰我，
但總比處於孤獨好得多。

溫蒂妮 繪

夏娃日記

No, he took no interest in my name.

I tried to hide my disappointment, but I suppose I did not succeed.

I went away and sat on the moss-bank with my feet in the water. It is where I go when I hunger for companionship, some one to look at, some one to talk to.

It is not enough—— that lovely white body painted there in the pool—— but it is something, and something is better than utter loneliness.

當我說話的時候，它就說話；當我悲傷時，它就悲傷；
它以憐憫的心情來安慰我，它說，
「你這沒有朋友可憐的小女孩，不要再覺得心灰意冷了，
我將是你的朋友。」
它是我的好朋友，唯一的一個，它是我的姊妹。

It talks when I talk; it is sad when I am sad; it comforts me
with its sympathy; it says, "Do not be downhearted, you poor
friendless girl; I will be your friend."
It is a good friend to me, and my only one; it is my sister.

一

我永遠不會忘記，她第一次離棄我，永遠永遠不會。

我的心像鉛塊一樣沈重，

我說，「她是我的所有，而她現在離開了！」

我絕望地說，「我的心都碎了，再也活不下去了。」

我用雙手摀著臉，非常的失望。

不過當我把雙手移開，

過了一會兒，她又出現了，

那個白皙、閃亮又美麗的女孩，

我跳入她的懷抱中！

一

That first time that she forsook me! ah, I shall never forget
that —— never, never.
My heart was lead in my body! I said, "She was all I had, and
now she is gone!" In my despair I said, "Break, my heart; I cannot
bear my life any more!" and hid my face in my hands, and there
was no solace for me.
And when I took them away, after a little, there she was again,
white and shining and beautiful, and I sprang into her arms!

那真是太幸福的感覺了，
我以前也知道幸福的滋味，但不像這一次，
這次讓我覺得非常非常的開心。
我再也不會對她起疑。
有時她離開了一下
或許一個小時，或許接近一天，
但我就是等待著、沒有任何懷疑。
我告訴自己，
「她在忙，或是她去旅行，她不久就會回來。」
事實上也是如此。她總是會回來。

當夜晚來臨，
如果天太黑，她就不會來，
因為她很膽小，
但若是有月亮，她就會出現。
我並不怕黑，
但是她的年紀比我小，比我晚出生；
我找過她很多很多次。
當我覺得傷心時，
她是我的安慰、我的避風港——
這是最主要的。

That was perfect happiness; I
had known happiness before,
but it was not like this, which
was ecstasy.
I never doubted her afterward.
Sometimes she stayed away——
maybe an hour, maybe almost
the whole day, but I waited and
did not doubt; I said, "She is
busy, or she is gone a journey,
but she will come."
And it was so: she always did.

At night she would not come if
it was dark, for she was a timid
little thing; but if there was a
moon she would come.
I am not afraid of the dark, but
she is younger than I am; she
was born after I was.
Many and many are the visits I
have paid her; she is my comfort
and my refuge when my life is
hard——and it is mainly that.

星期二

TUESDAY

整個早上我都忙著整理土地，故意的讓自己遠離他，
希望他會因為覺得寂寞而來找我，但是他並沒有。
到了中午，我完成早上的工作後，
就很開心的跟蜜蜂和蝴蝶在花叢間一起玩耍。
那些美麗的花朵能讓天上的神一直展現出微笑。
我收集那些美麗的花朵，把它們做成花圈和花環，
用它們來裝飾我自己。
然後我吃著午餐——當然是蘋果。
然後坐在蔭涼處，期望並等待著他的到來，但是他並沒有出現。

All the morning I was at work improving the estate; and I
purposely kept away from him in the hope that he would get
lonely and come. But he did not.
At noon I stopped for the day and took my recreation by flitting
all about with the bees and the butterflies and reveling in the
flowers, those beautiful creatures that catch the smile of God out
of the sky and preserve it!
I gathered them, and made them into wreaths and garlands and
clothed myself in them while I ate my luncheon —— apples, of
course; then I sat in the shade and wished and waited.
But he did not come.

—

不過沒關係，他有沒有出現都一樣，
因為他根本不喜歡花。
他把那些花稱為垃圾，根本不會區分不同種類的花，
並且還認為這樣比較能顯示出他自己的優越。
他不在意我、不在意那些花，
也不在意傍晚時被上了色的天空——
什麼是他在意的呢？
除了搭建棚子居住並隔絕美好並乾淨的雨水、
把瓜果打下來、品嘗葡萄、用手指撫弄樹上的水果，
以及看看那些水果的品質如何？

But no matter.
Nothing would have come of it, for he does not care
for flowers.
He called them rubbish, and cannot tell one from
another, and thinks it is superior to feel like that.
He does not care for me, he does not care for flowers,
he does not care for the painted sky at eventide——
is there anything he does care for, except building
shacks to coop himself up in from the good clean rain,
and thumping the melons, and sampling the grapes,
and fingering the fruit on the trees, to see how those
properties are coming along?

我把一根乾樹枝放在地上，
並試著用另一個樹枝在這根樹枝上鑽一個洞，
為了實現我的一個計畫。
沒多久，我嚇了一大跳，
一個有點細微的、透明的、
帶點藍色的薄霧從那洞中升起，
我把所有東西丟下，拔腿就跑。
我認為它是一個精靈，我實在太害怕了！
不過我回頭一看，它並沒有過來，
於是我靠著一塊大石頭，一邊休息一邊喘氣，
直到手腳不再發抖，我再躡手躡腳的回去。
並且小心謹慎的觀察，
準備一有任何問題就馬上飛奔離開。
當接近那裡，我撥開玫瑰枝叢偷看——
希望那個男人在附近，當時我看起來一定靈巧漂亮。
——不過精靈已經離開了。

—

I laid a dry stick on the ground and tried to bore a hole in it with another one, in order to carry out a scheme that I had, and soon I got an awful fright.

A thin, transparent bluish film rose out of the hole, and I dropped everything and ran!

I thought it was a spirit, and I was so frightened!

But I looked back, and it was not coming; so I leaned against a rock and rested and panted, and let my limbs go on trembling until they got steady again; then I crept warily back, alert, watching, and ready to fly if there was occasion; and when I was come near, I parted the branches of a rose-bush and peeped through —— wishing the man was about, I was looking so cunning and pretty —— but the sprite was gone.

我走過去，發現剛才我鑽的那個洞裡，
有一小撮細微的粉紅色粉末，我伸出手指想要碰觸它，
不自覺大叫了一聲「啊」，並趕快把手指移開。
我覺得手指非常的痛，
並把它含進嘴裡，邊跳邊叫著，
沒多久疼痛就減輕了，
然後我對這粉紅色的東西開始產生興趣並想要研究它。

I went there, and there was a pinch of
delicate pink dust in the hole.
I put my finger in, to feel it, and said OUCH!
And took it out again. It was a cruel pain.
I put my finger in my mouth; and by
standing first on one foot and then the other,
and grunting, I presently eased my misery;
then I was full of interest, and began to
examine.

我對這粉紅色的灰塵到底是什麼來歷到很好奇。
突然有一個名詞「火」，
靈光一現出現在我的腦海中，
雖然以前我從來沒有聽過。
我非常確定它就是如此稱呼，
因此便毫不遲疑地將它取名為「火」。

I was curious to know what the pink dust was.
Suddenly the name of it occurred to me, though I had
never heard of it before. It was FIRE!
I was as certain of it as a person could be
of anything in the world.
So without hesitation I named it that——fire.

我創造了一個以前在這世界上從不曾有過的東西，
我很確信我替這個世界無數的資源，
增加了一個新東西，並以此為傲，
並很想跑去找他，跟他說這件事，
想要提升我在他心中的重要性，
但是想想後，我還是放棄了，
因為他根本不會在意這些。
他還會問我，「這有什麼用？」
那我又該如何回答呢？
因為它一點用處也沒有，
只是很美麗，就只是很美麗罷了！

I had created something that didn't exist before; I had added a new thing to the world's uncountable properties; I realized this, and was proud of my achievement, and was going to run and find him and tell him about it, thinking to raise myself in his esteem—— but I reflected, and did not do it. No—— he would not care for it. He would ask what it was good for, and what could I answer? for if it was not good for something, but only beautiful, merely beautiful!

我嘆了一口氣，
沒有跑去找他，
因為這東西真的沒有任何用處，
它既不能拿來建造住處，
也不能用來改良瓜果，
也不能讓果實早點成熟，
真是一點用也沒有；
它真是一個沒用又蠢、華而不實的東西。
他會用一些很尖銳的字眼貶低它，
但是我對來說，它並不粗鄙低下。
我說，「喔，火，我愛你，
你這優美的粉紅色小東西，
你是這麼的美麗——這樣就夠了！」
我很想把它們全部擁入懷中，
但我沒這樣做。
然後我又發明了另一句跟第一句很相像的格言，
「被灼傷過的實驗品要避開火」，
我擔心可能有些瞟竊的嫌疑。

So I sighed, and did not go.
For it wasn't good for anything; it could not build a shack, it could not improve melons, it could not hurry a fruit crop; it was useless, it was a foolishness and a vanity; he would despise it and say cutting words.
But to me it was not despicable; I said, "Oh, you fire, I love you, you dainty pink creature, for you are BEAUTIFUL——and that is enough!" and was going to gather it to my breast.
But refrained. Then I made another maxim out of my head, though it was so nearly like the first one that I was afraid it was only a plagiarism: "THE BURNT EXPERIMENT SHUNS THE FIRE."

SMOKE

我又成功了。
當我弄了一堆火灰後，把它倒進一小撮乾稻草中，
打算把它帶回家玩時，
受到風的影響，它被噴散並猛烈的噴向我，
我馬上丟了它逃跑。
當我回頭看，
那藍色的精靈已經非常的高聳，
並且像雲一般不斷延伸，
我立刻就想到了一個名字——「煙」——
我敢保證，我以前從來沒聽過「煙」這個名字。

I wrought again; and when I had made a good deal of fire-dust I emptied it into a handful of dry brown grass, intending to carry it home and keep it always and play with it; but the wind struck it and it sprayed up and spat out at me fiercely, and I dropped it and ran.

When I looked back the blue spirit was towering up and stretching and rolling away like a cloud, and instantly I thought of the name of it——SMOKE ! ——though, upon my word, I had never heard of smoke before.

很快的，紅色和黃色的亮光從煙裡竄升出來，
我馬上將它們命名為「火焰」。
我是對的，雖然它們是這世界上最早的火焰。
那些火焰爬上了樹，
從大量而且越來越多、翻滾而上的濃煙中燦爛的閃耀著，
我非常開心地邊笑邊跳的手舞足蹈著，
這真是新鮮又特別，
而且既美好又美麗的景象啊！

Soon brilliant yellow and red flares shot up
through the smoke, and I named them in an instant
——FLAME——and I was right, too, though these
were the very first flames that had ever been in the
world.
They climbed the trees, then flashed splendidly in and
out of the vast and increasing volume of tumbling
smoke, and I had to clap my hands and laugh and
dance in my rapture, it was so new and strange and so
wonderful and so beautiful!

—

他跑過來凝視著，
並停在原地不動，好幾分鐘都說不出話。
接著他問，「這是什麼？」
唉，真是糟糕，
他問了一個這麼直接的問題。
當然，我要回答他，而我也回答了，
我說那是火。
如果因為我知道，而他卻必須問我的狀況
讓他不開心，
那也不是我的錯。
我並不想要讓他不開心。
過了一會兒，
他問，「它怎麼出現的？」
又是一個直接了當的問題，
我也只能直接的回答。
「我創造出來的。」

He came running, and stopped and gazed, and said not a word for many minutes.

Then he asked what it was.

Ah, it was too bad that he should ask such a direct question.

I had to answer it, of course, and I did. I said it was fire. If it annoyed him that I should know and he must ask; that was not my fault; I had no desire to annoy him.

After a pause he asked : "How did it come?"

Another direct question, and it also had to have a direct answer.

"I made it."

——

火勢越來越蔓延，

他走到被火燒過的地方的邊緣看著地面說，

「這些是什麼？」

「木炭。」

他拿起一塊木炭想要研究，

但改變了心意又把它放下，然後離開。

「沒有任何東西」可以引起他的興趣。

但是我很感興趣，

這些是木炭，灰色、柔軟、脆弱又美麗——我馬上知道它們是什麼。

還有餘燼，我也知道餘燼。

我發現了蘋果，非常開心地把它們從木炭堆中耙出來。

我還很年輕，食欲也很好。

不過我很失望，這些蘋果都迸開、壞掉了！

但表面上看起來壞了，事實上卻不是，

它們比生的蘋果更好吃。

火真是美麗，

我想有一天它一定會有用處！

The fire was travelling farther and farther off.
He went to the edge of the burned place and stood looking
down, and said:
"What are these?"
"Fire-coals."
He picked up one to examine it, but changed his mind and
put it down again. Then he went away.
NOTHING interests him.

But I was interested.

There were ashes, gray and soft and
delicate and pretty——I knew what they
were at once.

And the embers; I knew the embers, too.
I found my apples, and raked them out,
and was glad; for I am very young and
my appetite is active.

But I was disappointed; they were all
burst open and spoiled.

Spoiled apparently; but it was not so;
they were better than raw ones.

Fire is beautiful; some day it will be
useful, I think.

星期五

FRIDAY

我又看到他了！只有一會兒。
上星期一傍晚，但只看到了一下子！
我希望他會因為我好心的努力工作，並試著改善這塊土地
而稱讚我。
不過他並沒有高興，轉身就離開我了！
他曾經因為另一件事情對我感到不滿：
我再度試著勸告他不要再去那個瀑布。

I saw him again, for a moment, last Monday at nightfall, but only
for a moment.
I was hoping he would praise me for trying to improve the estate,
for I had meant well and had worked hard.
But he was not pleased, and turned away and left me.
He was also displeased on another account: I tried once more to
persuade him to stop going over the Falls.

—

那是因為火讓我感受到一種新的情緒——
相當新的感覺，跟愛、悲傷，
以及那些我已經知道的其他情感明顯的不同——害怕，
那真是很可怕——我希望永遠都不知道它，
它讓我掉入黑暗的時刻，破壞了我的快樂，
發抖、打顫並且直打哆嗦。
但是我勸不動他，他還沒體驗過害怕的感覺，
因此難以理解我的勸告。

—

That was because the fire had revealed to me a new passion——
quite new, and distinctly different from love, grief, and those
others which I had already discovered——FEAR.
And it is horrible!——I wish I had never discovered it; it gives
me dark moments, it spoils my happiness, it makes me shiver and
tremble and shudder.
But I could not persuade him, for he has not discovered fear yet,
and so he could not understand me.

星期二、星期三、星期四，
還有今天，
我都沒有看見他，
孤單一人的時間總是漫長，
不過孤單一人總比不受歡迎好。

Tuesday —— Wednesday —— Thursday ——
and today: all without seeing him.
It is a long time to be alone; still, it is better to be alone
than unwelcome.

我必須要有同伴——我想我就是這樣的構造——
因此我跟動物們交朋友。
牠們很迷人，而且牠們的性情溫和、行為優雅，
牠們從來不會看起來不開心，從不會讓你覺得你打擾了牠們。
牠們會對你笑並搖著尾巴，如果牠們有任何一個表現，
代表牠們已準備好跟你去玩耍或郊遊，或是你想要做的任何事；
我認為牠們是很棒的紳士。
這些日子以來，我們一起共度很棒的時光，
從來沒有覺得寂寞。寂寞！不，我沒有！

I had to have company —— I was made for it, I think —— so I made
friends with the animals.
They are just charming, and they have the kindest disposition and
the politest ways; they never look sour, they never let you feel that
you are intruding, they smile at you and wag their tail, if they've
got one, and they are always ready for a romp or an excursion or
anything you want to propose.
I think they are perfect gentlemen.
All these days we have had such good times, and it hasn't been
lonesome for me, ever.
Lonesome! No, I should say not.

為什麼？
牠們總是有一大群圍繞在我周邊——
有時多到佔據了四、五畝的面積——
根本難以計算有多少數量。
當你站在岩石上，
眺望動物們那閃耀著光澤、色彩斑斕的皮毛時，
會覺得那些毛皮的波動，就像湖面被吹皺時的線條，
但你知道那並不是。
還有喜好社交的鳥兒成群結隊、如颶風般呼呼的鼓動翅膀，
當陽光灑在這些騷動的羽毛，
你會覺得這些色彩像是要燃燒起來，足以讓你目眩神迷。

Why, there's always a swarm of them around —— sometimes as
much as four or five acres —— you can't count them; and when
you stand on a rock in the midst and look out over the furry
expanse, it is so mottled and splashed and gay with color and
frisking sheen and sun-flash, and so rippled with stripes, that
you might think it was a lake, only you know it isn't; and there's
storms of sociable birds, and hurricanes of whirring wings; and
when the sun strikes all that feathery commotion, you have a blazing
up of all the colors you can think of, enough to put your eyes out.

我們經歷了一個漫長的旅行，
我看過世界大部分的地方——幾乎全部。
我想，我是第一位旅行者，也是唯一的一位。
當我們行進時，那景象非常壯觀，沒有任何行進隊伍像我們這樣。
騎在老虎或豹的身上比較舒服，
因為牠們比較柔軟又有一個適合我乘坐的圓背，
而且牠們是非常漂亮的動物。
不過如果是長途的旅程
或是想要看風景，
我就會騎乘在大象的背上。
大象會用牠的鼻子把我舉起來，
但我可以自己下來；
當我們準備紮營，
牠會坐下來，
讓我從牠的背上滑下來。

We have made long excursions, and I have see a great deal of the world——almost all of it, I think; and so I am the first traveller, and the only one.

When we are on the march, it is an imposing sight——there's nothing like it anywhere.

For comfort I ride a tiger or a leopard, because it is soft and has a round back that fits me, and because they are such pretty animals; but for long distance or for scenery I ride the elephant.

He hoists me up with his trunk, but I can get off myself; when we are ready to camp, he sits and I slide down the back way.

——

鳥兒和動物們彼此都非常的友善，沒有任何的爭執。
牠們彼此聊天、也跟我聊天，但牠們的語言一定是外國話，
因為我完全不了解牠們在說什麼；
但是剛我跟牠們交談時，牠們卻能了解我的意思，
尤其是狗和大象。
這讓我覺得很不好意思，表示牠們比我聰明，比我高等。
這讓我不怎麼開心，因為我希望自己是主要的實驗品，
而我也打算變成如此。

——

The birds and animals are all friendly to each other, and there are no
disputes about anything.
They all talk, and they all talk to me, but it must be a foreign language,
for I cannot make out a word they say; yet they often understand me
when I talk back, particularly the dog and the elephant.
It makes me ashamed. It shows that they are brighter than I am ,and
are therefore my superiors.
It annoys me, for I want to be the principal Experiment
myself——and I intend to be, too.

———

我學了許多東西，
現在我是受過教育的，但一開始並不是。
剛開始我是無知的，一開始我常會感到困擾，
因為不管觀察多久，
我總覺得自己不夠聰明，所以從來沒看過水往上流，
但現在我不在意了。
經過不斷的實驗，我知道水永遠不會往上流，
除非在黑夜中。
我知道水在黑夜中才會往上流，
因為水池的水從來都沒有乾涸，
當然，水還是會乾涸，如果水在黑夜沒有流回來。
最好能藉由真正的實驗來證明事情，
然後你才能真正明瞭；
如果只是藉由猜測、假設和推測，
那你永遠都不能獲得知識。

I have learned a number of things, and am educated, now, but I wasn't at first. I was ignorant at first. At first it used to vex me because, with all my watching, I was never smart enough to be around when the water was running uphill; but now I do not mind it. I have experimented and experimented until now I know it never does run uphill, except in the dark.

I know it does in the dark, because the pool never goes dry; which it would, of course, if the water didn't come back in the night.

It is best to prove things by actual experiment; then you know; whereas if you depend on guessing and supposing and conjecturing, you never get educated.

有些事情你沒辦法找到答案，不過光憑著推測和猜想，
你並不能知道自己找不到答案，你必須有耐心地繼續做實驗，
直到你發現答案找不到為止。
經由這樣的過程找到解答是讓人開心的，
也是這個世界之所以如此有趣的原因。
如果沒有任何事情可探尋，那將是無趣的。
即便發現找不到答案，也跟找到答案同樣有趣，不，也許更有趣。
水的祕密就像是一個寶藏，直到我發現了它，
然後興奮就全部消失了，並體會到一股失落感。

Some things you can't find out; but you will never know you can't by guessing and supposing:
no, you have to be patient and go on experimenting until you find out that you can't find out. And it is delightful to have it that way, it makes the world so interesting.
If there wasn't anything to find out, it would be dull.
Even trying to find out and not finding out is just as interesting as trying to find out and finding out, and I don't know but more so.
The secret of the water was a treasure until I got it; then the excitement all went away, and I recognized a sense of loss.

——

從實驗中我知道，木頭會游泳，還有枯葉、羽毛，以及很多其他東西；
因此從這一連串的例證你知道石頭會游泳，
但是你必須停留在單純的知道層面，沒有任何方法可以證明──
到現在為止。
不過我會找到方法的，然後那種興奮又會消失。
諸如此類的事情讓我覺得很難過，
因為當每一個東西慢慢地都被我發現，我就不再有興奮感，
而我又是那麼的喜歡有興奮的感覺！
有一天晚上我就因為想著這件事而睡不著覺。

——

By experiment I know that wood swims, and dry leaves,
and feathers, and plenty of other things; therefore by all that
cumulative evidence you know that a rock will swim; but you
have to put up with simply knowing it, for there isn't any way to
prove it——up to now.
But I shall find a way——then that excitement will go.
Such things make me sad; because by and by when I have found
out everything there won't be any more excitements, and I do
love excitements so!
The other night I couldn't sleep for thinking about it.

——

起初，我不能理解自己為何被創造出來？
但是現在我認為我之所以來到這個世上，
就是要找出存在於這個美妙世界中的奧秘，
並能因而感到快樂
以及感謝造物主所制定的這一切。
我想還有許多東西要學習——我希望如此；
我想我要節制一點、不要太著急，
還有很多東西讓我一步步學習，
我希望如此。

——

At first I couldn't make out what I was made for, but now I
think it was to search out the secrets of this wonderful world
and be happy and thank the Giver of it all for devising it.
I think there are many things to learn yet——I hope so; and
by economizing and not hurrying too fast I think they will last
weeks and weeks. I hope so.

當你拋出一根羽毛，它會在空氣中滑翔再慢慢消失，
然而當你丟出一個石塊，
卻不會這樣，每一次石塊都會掉下來；
我嘗試了一次又一次都是如此。
為什麼會這樣呢？
當然它並不是掉下來，但為什麼看起來像是掉下來呢？
我猜可能是視覺上的錯覺。
我的意思是，羽毛和石塊其中一個有一個是視覺上造成的問題，
我不知道是哪一個，
可能是羽毛，可能是石塊；
我沒辦法證明是哪一個，
只能示範出兩者之一有一個是假象，
然後就讓人自己選擇吧！

When you cast up a feather it sails away on the air and goes out of sight; then you throw up a clod and it doesn't.
It comes down, every time. I have tried it and tried it, and it is always so.
I wonder why it is?
Of course it doesn't come down, but why should it seem to?
I suppose it is an optical illusion.
I mean, one of them is.
I don't know which one.
It may be the feather, it may be the clod; I can't prove which it is, I can only demonstrate that one or the other is a fake, and let a person take his choice.

藉由觀察，我知道星星並不是一直存在著，
我曾經看過一些很棒的星星融化並從天空掉落；
既然有一顆星星會融化，那就表示所有的星星都會融化，
既然它們都會融化，就可以在同一個晚上全部融化。
我了解這種讓人悲傷的事情早晚會發生，
所以我打算每天晚上只要還是清醒著，
就要坐著看那些星星，
而且要把那些閃閃發亮的景象深深記在腦海中，
以便等晚些時候它們被拿走時，我可以按照自己的喜好，
把那些可愛的、一大片的星星還原到夜空中，
讓它們再次的閃閃發光，而我的淚水所造成的模糊視線，
會讓那些星星的數量看起來更加倍。

By watching, I know that the stars are not going to last.
I have seen some of the best ones melt and run down the sky.
Since one can melt, they can all melt; since they can all melt,
they can all melt the same night.
That sorrow will come——I know it. I mean to sit up every
night and look at them as long as I can keep awake; and I will
impress those sparkling field on my memory, so that by and
by when they are taken away I can by my fancy restore those
lovely myriads to the black sky and make them sparkle again,
and double them by the blur of my tears.

在墮落之後

AFTER THE FALL

當我回想從前，
那個花園對我來說像是一場夢，
它很美，非常的美！
無與倫比的美麗！
但它現在不存在了，
我再也看不到它了！

When I look back, the Garden
is a dream to me.
It was beautiful, surpassingly
beautiful, enchantingly
beautiful; and now it is lost,
and I shall not see it any more.

雖然我失去了花園，但是我發現了「他」！我很滿足！
他盡其所能的愛我，而我也滿懷熱情的愛他，
我想對我這樣的年輕女性而言，這樣的結果是適合的。
如果我問自己為什麼愛他？
我發現自己並不知道，也不是很想知道，
因此我猜想這種愛並不可以用任何理由和統計可以說明，
也不同於一個人對其他的爬蟲類和動物的愛，
我想一定是這樣。

The Garden is lost, but I have found HIM, and am content.
He loves me as well as he can; I love him with all the strength
of my passionate nature, and this, I think, is proper to my
youth and sex.
If I ask myself why I love him, I find I do not
know, and do not really much care to know;
so I suppose that this kind of love is not a
product of reasoning and statistics, like
one's love for other reptiles and animals.
I think that this must be so.

我喜歡某些種類的鳥，
因為牠們的歌聲，
但我愛亞當並不是因為他的歌聲——
不，並不是因為這樣。
他的歌聲很糟，讓我受不了，
但我還是要求他唱歌，
因為我希望學著喜歡他有興趣的事情。
我相信我可以做得到，因為一開始我難以忍受，但現在可以了！
他的歌聲會讓牛奶變酸，
但沒關係，我可以讓自己習慣喝那種牛奶。

I love certain birds because of their song; but I do not love
Adam on account of his singing — no, it is not that.
The more he sings the more I do not get reconciled to it.
Yet I ask him to sing, because I wish to learn to like everything
he is interested in. I am sure I can learn, because at first I could
not stand it, but now I can.
It sours the milk, but it doesn't matter; I can get used to that
kind of milk.

———

我並不是因為他聰明而愛他——不，不是的。
他並不能歸咎自己不夠聰明，
因為他不能決定這件事，
是上帝把他製造成這樣，如此就可以了；
不聰明有不聰明的優點，我很了解這點。
而且隨著時間的流逝，他會越來越聰明，
雖然我認為這樣的改變不會突然發生，
但是不用急，他現在這個樣子就很不錯了。

———

It is not on account of his brightness that I love him——no, it is
not that.
He is not to blame for his brightness, such as it is, for he did not
make it himself; he is as God make him, and that is sufficient.
There was a wise purpose in it, that I know.
In time it will develop, though I think it will not be sudden; and
besides, there is no hurry; he is well enough just as he is.

———

我愛他並不是因為他的親切、體貼和敏感，

事實上他在這些方面是有所欠缺的，

但他現在這樣就已經很不錯了，而且會越來越好。

我並不是因為他的勤奮而愛上他——不，不是這樣。

我想他應該有這種特性，

但我不知道他為何在我面前要將它隱藏起來，這是我唯一的痛，

除此之外，現在他對我都很坦白，

我確定除了這件事外，他對我沒有任何隱瞞。

———

It is not on account of his gracious and considerate ways and his delicacy that I love him.

No, he has lacks in these regards, but he is well enough just so, and is improving.

It is not on account of his industry that I love him——no, it is not that. I think he has it in him, and I do not know why he conceals it from me. It is my only pain.

Otherwise he is frank and open with me, now. I am sure he keeps nothing from me but this.

他有祕密不讓我知道讓我覺得難過，
有時我會因為想到這件事而失眠，
但我盡量不去想，
而這件事不會影響我現在幸福滿溢的生活。
我並不是因為他的學識而愛他——
不，並不是這樣。
他完全是靠自學的，並且懂得很多事情，
但這並不是我愛他的原因。

It grieves me that he should have a secret from me, and
sometimes it spoils my sleep, thinking of it, but I will put it
out of my mind; it shall not trouble my happiness, which is
otherwise full to overflowing.
It is not on account of his education that I love him —— no, it
is not that.
He is self-educated, and does really know a multitude of
things, but they are not so.

我不是因為他的騎士精神而愛上他——不，不是這樣。
他說我的壞話，但是我不怪他，
我想這是不同性別的特質，但他並不能選擇自己的性別。
當然，我不會說他的壞話，
若果真如此我會先滅亡，那也是因為性別不同所致，
我不能因而居功，因為性別不是我自己能決定的。

 It is not on account of his chivalry that I love
him ——no, it is not that.
He told on me, but I do not blame him; it is
a peculiarity of sex, I think, and he did not
make his sex.
Of course I would not have told on him,
I would have perished first; but that is a
peculiarity of sex, too, and I do not take
credit for it, for I did not make my sex.

—

那我到底為什麼愛他？

我想只是因為「他是一個男人」吧！

他的本性很好，我因為這點愛上他，

但他如果不是這樣，我也還是愛他；

我知道，即便他打我、罵我，我還是一樣愛他

我很清楚這點。

我想，這是因為天性吧！

Then why is it that I love him?
MERELY BECAUSE HE IS MASCULINE, I think.
At bottom he is good, and I love him for that, but I could love
him without it.
If he should beat me and abuse me, I should go on loving him.
I know it.
It is a matter of sex, I think.

——

他強壯又英俊，我因此而愛上他，
我仰慕他並以他為傲，
不過如果他沒有這些特質，我還是會一樣愛他。
如果他平凡無奇，我愛他；
如果他很虛弱，我還是愛他。
我會為他工作，當他的奴隸，為他禱告，
待在他的床邊看他，直到我死。

▬

He is strong and handsome, and I love
him for that, and I admire him and
am proud of him, but I could love him
without those qualities.
If he he were plain, I should love him; if
he were a wreck, I should love him; and
I would work for him, and slave over
him, and pray for him, and watch by
his bedside until I died.

——

是的，我想我愛他，只因為他是我的，他是男人，
大概沒有其他的理由。
我想就像我一開始說的，
這種愛並不是任何理由和統計的產物，
它就這樣不知不覺地出現，而且難以解釋也不需要解釋。
這些是我的看法，但我只是一個女孩，
又是第一個探討這件事，
有可能因為我的疏忽和缺乏經驗而把事情搞錯了！

——

Yes, I think I love him merely because he is MINE and is MASCULINE.
There is no other reason, I suppose. And so I think it is as I first said: that this kind of love is not a product of reasonings and statistics.
It just comes——none knows whence——and cannot explain itself. And doesn't need to.
It is what I think. But I am only a girl, and the first that has examined this matter, and it may turn out that in my ignorance and inexperience I have not got it right.

四十年以後

FORTY YEARS LATER

我祈禱並期盼我們可以攜手共度一生——
這個期盼永遠不會從地球上消失，
並會長存於每一個深愛丈夫的妻子心中，
直到歲月的盡頭——我以我的名字為禱告。
如果有一個人必須要先離開這個世界，我祈禱那個人是我；
因為他是堅強的，而我是軟弱的，我對他來說並不是必要的，
但他對我卻是必要的——沒有他的日子就不再是生活，
我怎麼能夠忍受？這個祈禱是永遠的，
只要有我的族群存在的一天，這個祈求就會永久的傳下去。
我是第一個妻子，在最後一個妻子中，我將被複製。

It is my prayer, it is my longing, that we may pass from this life
together —— a longing which shall never perish from the earth,
but shall have place in the heart of every wife that loves, until the
end of time; and it shall be called by my name.
But if one of us must go first, it is my prayer that it shall be I; for
he is strong, I am weak, I am not so necessary to him as he is to
me —— life without him would not be life; how could I endure it?
This prayer is also immortal, and will not cease from being
offered up while my race continues. I am the first wife; and in the
last wife I shall be repeated.

在夏娃的墓前

AT EVE'S GRAVE

亞當：夏娃在哪裡，哪裡就是伊甸園。

ADAM: Wheresoever she was, THERE was Eden.

摘錄自亞當的日記

EXTRACT FROM ADAM'S DIARY

—

或許我應該要記得她還很小、
只是一個小女孩，要多體諒她。
她充滿了好奇、熱忱以及活力，
這世界對她而言是迷人的、美妙的、神祕的、喜悅的。
當發現了一種新的花朵，她無法只用言語來形容她的喜悅。
她必須愛撫它、照顧它、聞聞它，
跟它說說話，並對著它們說一些可愛的名字。

—

Perhaps I ought to remember that she is very young, a mere girl and make allowances.
She is all interest, eagerness, vivacity, the world is to her a charm, a wonder, a mystery, a joy; she can't speak for delight when she finds a new flower, she must pet it and caress it and smell it and talk to it, and pour out endearing names upon it.

─

而且她對顏色有狂熱，
棕色的石頭、黃色的沙、灰色的泥沼、藍色的天空，
以及如珍珠般的黎明、山上紫色的影子、夕陽西下時，
漂浮在被染紅的海洋上的金色小島、蒼白的月亮滑過細碎的雲朵、
如珍珠般的星星在天際邊閃爍——這些事物就我來看，
都沒有什麼實際的價值，但因為它們多彩又莊嚴，
對她而言就足夠了。
她為它們而痴狂。

▬

And she is color-mad: brown rocks, yellow
sand, gray moss, green foliage, blue sky; the
pearl of the dawn, the purple shadows on
the mountains, the golden islands floating
in crimson seas at sunset, the pallid moon
sailing through the shredded cloud-rack,
the star-jewels glittering in the wastes
of space —— none of them is of any
practical value, so far as I can see, but
because they have color and majesty, that
is enough for her, and she loses her mind
over them.

如果她能夠保持安靜並一次維持數分鐘不動，
那將是多麼安詳的景象，那麼我想我就會樂於注視著她，
我確定我會這麼做。
因為我漸漸發現她是一個非常引人注目又美麗的傢伙──
輕盈、纖細、豐滿、美麗、伶俐、優雅。
有一次她如大理石般潔白的站在大圓石上，
陽光灑滿了她全身，她的頭微微向後，並用手遮蔽陽光，
看著飛翔在天空的鳥兒，我承認她是美麗的。

If she could quiet down and keep still a couple minutes at a time,
it would be a reposeful spectacle.
In that case I think I could enjoy looking at her; indeed I am sure
I could, for I am coming to realize that she is a quite remarkably
comely creature——lithe, slender, trim, rounded, shapely, nimble,
graceful; and once when she was standing marble-white and sun-
drenched on a bowlder, with her young head tilted back and her
hand shading her eyes, watching the flight of a bird in
the sky, I recognized that she was beautiful.

星期一中午

MONDAY NOON

——

如果這個星球上有任何一樣東西是她不感興趣的，
那麼那樣東西就不是我所知道的。
我對某些動物並不感興趣，但是對她而言卻未必如此。
她跟牠們都很親近，沒有任何歧視與差別，
她認為牠們都是寶藏，並歡迎每一個新來的成員。

——

If there is anything on the planet that she is not
interested in it is not in my list.
There are animals that I am indifferent to, but it is not
so with her.
She has no discrimination, she takes to all of them,
she thinks they are all treasures, every new one is
welcome.

當巨大的雷龍大步走進園子時，
她將牠的到來視為一種收穫，
我則認為是一個災難，
這是我們對事物的看法總是缺乏共識的最好例子。
她想要馴養牠，
我則想要搬出這裡，
把這裡當成禮物送給那隻雷龍！

When the mighty brontosaurus
came striding into camp, she
regarded it as an acquisition, I
considered it a calamity; that is a
good sample of the lack of harmony
that prevails in our views of things.
She wanted to domesticate it, I
wanted to make it a present of the
homestead and move out.

她認為可以用溫和的方式馴服牠，
使牠成為一隻很棒的寵物。
我說，「一隻二十一英呎高、
八十四英呎長的寵物，並不適合待在這個地方。」
因為即便牠沒有任何傷害人的意圖，
也有可能因為坐下來而壓壞房子，
不管是誰，只要光看牠的眼神，
就可以知道牠呆呆的。

She believed it could be tamed by kind
treatment and would be a good pet; I said
a pet twenty-one feet high and eighty-four
feet long would be no proper thing to have
about the place, because, even with the best
intentions and without meaning any harm,
it could sit down on the house and mash it,
for any one could see by the look of its eye
that it was absent-minded.

然而，她還是下定決心要養這隻怪物，毫不放棄。
她認為我們可以從牠開始經營酪農業，
並要我幫忙擠奶，但我不肯，那太危險了。
我們連牠是什麼性別都不知道，也沒有任何梯子。
然後她又想要騎著牠看風景。
牠擺放在地上的尾巴有三十或四十英呎長，就像一棵倒下的樹。
然後她認為可以從尾巴爬到牠身上，但是她錯了，
當她爬到陡峭的地方時，因為太滑而掉下來，
幸好有我，否則她可能會受傷。

Still, her heart was set upon having that monster, and she
couldn't give it up.
She thought we could start a dairy with it, and wanted me to
help milk it; but I wouldn't; it was too risky. The sex wasn't right,
and we hadn't any ladder anyway.
Then she wanted to ride it, and look at the scenery.
Thirty or forty feet of its tail was lying on the ground, like a
fallen tree, and she thought she could climb it, but she was
mistaken; when she got to the steep place it was too slick and
down she came, and would have hurt herself but for me.

那她滿足了嗎？

不，除了實際的驗證外，任何東西都不會讓她滿足！

未經實驗的理論是不會被她接受的，她不接受它們！

這種精神是正確的，我承認，這很吸引我，

我感受到這所產生的影響，如果我有更多時間跟她在一起，

我想我會受到影響。

Was she satisfied now?
No. Nothing ever satisfies her but demonstration; untested
theories are not in her line, and she won't have them.
It is the right spirit, I concede it; it attracts me; I
feel the influence of it; if I were with her more I
think I should take it up myself.

嗯，關於這隻巨物，她還有一個理論：

如果我們能馴服牠，讓牠很友善，就能讓牠站在河中當成一座橋。

牠其實已經很溫馴了——至少對她而言——

因此她試著嘗試她的理論，但是失敗了。

每次當她讓牠站在河中，然後自己走回岸上，

想要從牠的背上過河時，

牠便跟著她一起從河中走出、跟在她身旁，像一座寵物山。

動物其實就是這樣，牠們都會這樣。

Well, she had one theory remaining about this colossus:
she thought that if we could tame it and make him friendly we
could stand in the river and use him for a bridge.
It turned out that he was already plenty tame enough——at least
as far as she was concerned——so she tried her theory, but it
failed: every time she got him properly placed in the river and
went ashore to cross over him, he came out and followed her
around like a pet mountain. Like the other animals.
They all do that.

夏娃日記 Eve's diary

作　　　者	/馬克吐溫
繪　　　者	/溫蒂妮
企　　　劃	/張曉蕊
責 任 編 輯	/張曉蕊
版　　　權	/黃淑敏、翁靜如
行 銷 業 務	/周佑潔、張倚禎

總　編　輯	/陳美靜
總　經　理	/彭之琬
發　行　人	/何飛鵬
法 律 顧 問	/台英國際商務法律事務所
出　　　版	/商周出版
	台北市中山區民生東路二段141號9樓
	電話：(02) 2500-7008　　傳真：(02) 2500-7759
	E-mail：bwp.service@cite.com.tw
發　　　行	/英屬蓋曼群島商家庭傳媒股份有限公司　城邦分公司
	台北市中山區民生東路二段141號2樓
	電話：(02) 2500-0888　　傳真：(02) 2500-1938
	讀者服務專線：0800-020-299　　24小時傳真服務：(02) 2517-0999
	讀者服務信箱：service@readingclub.com.tw
	劃撥帳號：19833503
	戶名：英屬蓋曼群島商家庭傳媒股份有限公司　城邦分公司
香港發行所	/城邦（香港）出版集團有限公司
	香港灣仔駱克道193號東超商業中心1樓
	電話：(852) 2508-6231　　傳真：(852) 2578-9337
	E-mail：hkcite@biznetvigator.com
馬新發行所	/城邦（馬新）出版集團
	Cite (M) Sdn Bhd
	41, Jalan Radin Anum, Bandar Baru Sri Petaling,
	57000 Kuala Lumpur, Malaysia.
	電話：(603) 9057-8822　　傳真：(603) 9057-6622
	E-mail：cite@cite.com.my

印　　　刷	/鴻霖印刷傳媒有限公司
總　經　銷	/高見文化行銷股份有限公司
	電話：(02) 2668-9005　　傳真：(02) 2668-9790
	客服專線：0800-055-365

■ 2014年（民103）12月初版
ISBN 978-986-272-714-0

城邦讀書花園
www.cite.com.tw

國家圖書館出版品預行編目（CIP）資料

夏娃日記／馬克吐溫著；溫蒂妮繪.
-- 初版. -- 臺北市：商周出版：
家庭傳媒城邦分公司發行, 民103.12
　　面；　　公分

ISBN 978-986-272-714-0（平裝）

874.57　　　　　　　103023903

定價280元